The Case of the Terrible T. rex

(and Other Super-Scientific Cases)

MICHELE T

ILLUSTRATE
BARBARA JOHANSE

T. REX

STERLING CHILDREN'S BOOKS
New York

To the brilliant, beautiful, wise,
and talented Illustrious M. You rock!

A bajillion thanks to Harry Howell, the ultimate ham,
for his patient help with all things radio related.
(Hams can chat with Harry at KA7ECY.)

M. T.

For Mike, my scientist son

B. J. N.

STERLING CHILDREN'S BOOKS
New York

An Imprint of Sterling Publishing
387 Park Avenue South
New York, NY 10016

STERLING CHILDREN'S BOOKS and the distinctive Sterling Children's Books logo are trademarks of
Sterling Publishing Co., Inc.

Text © 2010 by Michele Torrey
Illustrations © 2010 by Barbara Johansen Newman

ISBN 978-1-4027-4966-7

Distributed in Canada by Sterling Publishing
c/o Canadian Manda Group, 165 Dufferin Street
Toronto, Ontario, Canada M6K 3H6
Distributed in the United Kingdom by GMC Distribution Services
Castle Place, 166 High Street, Lewes, East Sussex, England BN7 1XU
Distributed in Australia by Capricorn Link (Australia) Pty. Ltd.
P.O. Box 704, Windsor, NSW 2756, Australia

For information about custom editions, special sales, and premium and
corporate purchases, please contact Sterling Special Sales at 800-805-5489
or specialsales@sterlingpublishing.com.

Manufactured in The United States of America
Lot#:
2 4 6 8 10 9 7 5 3
08/12

The ARES® logo is a registered trademark of ARRL, the National Association
for Amateur Radio™. Used by permission. All rights reserved.

CONTENTS

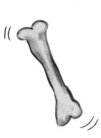

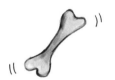

CHAPTER ONE
Midnight in Mossy Lake

The light of the full moon shone on the small town of Mossy Lake. It shone on the town's square, where the clock chimed midnight. It shone on Ted's Barber Shop, where a mouse nibbled on a crumb. It shone on Barbarella's Dance Studio, where for just twelve dollars you could learn to waltz or even tango.

Not least of all, the light of the full moon shone down upon a particular house. And standing at a particular attic window, staring back at the moon through a telescope, was a boy. His name was Drake Doyle, and he was a scientist. Not a mad scientist, mind you, but a most excellent scientist indeed. His cinnamon toast-colored hair stood straight up. He wore a white lab coat with his name on it.

Drake whipped a pencil out from behind his ear and scribbled in his lab notebook:

As I suspected.
Hypothesis correct.
Green cheese: negative.

Just then, the phone rang.

Now, in case you're wondering who could be calling at midnight, wonder no more. You see, Drake was also a detective. And science detectives are on call 24/7. Drake's business cards read:

Doyle and Fossey:
Science Detectives
call us. anytime. 555-7822

Nell Fossey was Drake's business partner. Whether the case involved ghosts or garbage, penguins or parades, they were on it. No problem was too big or too small for Doyle and Fossey, the best science detectives in the fifth grade.

"Doyle and Fossey," Drake answered.

"Detective Doyle? It's me, Wiley."

"Ah yes, Mr. Wiley Millard." Wiley was in Drake's class at school and was a whiz at video games. He could put dozens of dragons to sleep

2

at once. He could parachute into the Congo and rescue lost explorers. He could save little old ladies from armies of vampires—all while sitting on his couch. "What seems to be the trouble?" Drake asked.

"I'm camping on Waxberry Hill with my dad."

"Lovely night for camping," said Drake.

"Hardly," griped Wiley. "You see, my dad *made* me come camping. He said I spend way too much time playing video games and need to learn how to appreciate nature."

"Excellent advice," said Drake, whose partner, Nell, happened to appreciate nature very much.

"Not so excellent. I'm in my tent. My dad's sound asleep, but I can't sleep a wink. Something's howling out there. I think—I think it's a *werewolf*, and I don't have my joystick!"

Drake was so shocked that he dropped his lab notebook. A werewolf! Horrors! One bite from a werewolf, and, well, you became a werewolf yourself. If Wiley was right . . . if there really was a werewolf on Waxberry Hill . . . well, the thought was too horrifying to imagine!

"I understand if you're too scared," Wiley was saying. "Not everyone's a werewolf warrior. I'll call Frisco . . . he likes to destroy things."

Egads! thought Drake, doubly horrified. *Not James Frisco!* Frisco was in the science detective business, too. But unlike Drake and Nell, Frisco was a bad scientist . . . a *mad* scientist, scientifically speaking. Instead of stirring a solution according to the instructions, Frisco said, "Stirring, schmirring. Waste of time." Instead of recording everything in his lab notebook, Frisco said, "Notebook, schmotebook. Notebooks are for geeks." And instead of turning everything off in his laboratory before leaving, Frisco said, "Off, schmoff. Who cares anyway?" His business cards read:

```
FRISCO
b̶a̶d̶ mad scientist
(Better than Doyle and Fossey)
Call me. Day or night. 555-6190
```

Drake could never let Frisco handle this most horrifying case. "You're in luck, Mr. Millard!" said Drake. "Last week I bought a Detect-O-Werewolf Gizmo Gadget! Guaranteed to detect a werewolf or your money back. We'll take the case!"

Immediately, Drake phoned Nell.

"Doyle and Fossey," she answered.

"Werewolf wailing on Waxberry Hill. Wiley waiting for wescue—I—I mean, *rescue*. No time to lose. I'll pick you up in ten minutes."

"Check."

Click.

The second Drake and his dad pulled up in front of Nell's house, Nell hopped into the backseat. She was the best partner a science detective could have. (Not to mention being Drake's best friend.) She wore a backpack that Drake knew was filled with handy gadgets. Her coffee-colored hair was pulled back into a no-nonsense ponytail. Drake knew she meant business. Scientific business of the no-nonsense sort. "Waxberry Hill, Mr. Doyle," Nell said. "Double time!"

"Check," said Mr. Doyle.

Drake and Nell hung on as tires squealed.

Through town, over Plum River, through Fernfiddle Forest . . . it was a long way to Waxberry Hill.

Lucky for them, Mr. Sam Doyle was at the wheel. You see, Mr. Doyle was a scientist himself. He owned his own science equipment and supply company. He made certain that Drake and Nell never ran out of test tubes, sharpened pencils, or lab coats with their names on them. And if business called them out late at night? When the moon was full, and the clock had already struck midnight? When a werewolf was on the prowl? No question. Mr. Doyle was their man.

The clock in the town's square had barely struck one o'clock by the time Mr. Doyle parked next to the Millards' truck near Waxberry Hill. The three of them jumped out of the car and hurried up the trail to the campsite.

CHAPTER TWO
A Most
Horrible Howl

The moon hovered over Wiley's tent. A steamy mist swirled between rocks and thorny brambles. Eyes gleamed from the bushes.

"Creepy," whispered Nell.

"Spooky," Drake replied.

Mr. Doyle sat on a log and unfolded a newspaper. His headlamp illuminated the pages. "Scream if you need me," he said, stifling a yawn.

Drake scanned the area with his Detect-O-Werewolf Gizmo Gadget. "All systems clear," he said to Nell. "Lucky for us, the werewolf must be taking a break. Tired of howling, perhaps."

"Hmm." Nell sniffed the air. "Peculiar odor. Like eggs, only stinkier."

"Hmm . . . right as usual, Scientist Nell. Stinky

eggs. Odd. Very odd. Perhaps the werewolf is having an after-midnight snack."

Drake and Nell approached Wiley's tent.

"Knock, knock," said Drake.

"Who's there?" Wiley opened the flap.

"Doyle and Fossey at your service." Nell handed Wiley their business card.

"Mind if we take a look inside?" asked Drake.

Wiley frowned. "But what about the were-wolf? Aren't you going to capture him? If I were at home, I would have blasted him to smithereens by now. He wouldn't stand a chance."

"First things first," said Nell. "All good scientists must make observations before they can draw conclusions."

And so the science detectives got to work. They whipped out their lab notebooks and their pencils. They shone their headlamps around.

"Wiley's dad, Mr. Millard, is in his sleeping bag," observed Nell. "He appears to be a very sound sleeper." As if to prove Nell's point, Mr. Millard rolled over and gave a little snort, followed by a snuffle and a snore.

Drake pushed up his glasses. "I couldn't help observing that the tent is rather lopsided and not staked down very well."

"My dad made me pitch the tent myself. I got tangled in a thorn bush but finally did it." Wiley frowned. "I hate tents. I hate camping. This is stupid, and we're all going to turn into werewolves if you guys don't put it into hyperspeed."

"Mm-hmm, yes, yes, I see." Drake scribbled a note to himself: *Wiley's dad out like a light, tent lopsided, Wiley tangled in thorn bush, nature appreciation lesson a failure.*

"The smell of stinky eggs is especially strong in here," said Nell.

Wiley's eyes widened. "It's the stench of the werewolf."

Nell fanned her face with her lab notebook. "Not only is it stinkier in here, but have you noticed it's getting steamy and hot?"

"Excellent observation, Scientist Nell." Drake wrote: *Tent stinky, and getting steamier and hotter by the second.* "Now, tell me, Mr. Millard," said Drake, dabbing his forehead with a hankie. "When did you first hear the howling?"

"Right after we hit the sack," Wiley said. "Dad fell asleep right away, but I couldn't get comfortable. That's when I heard—"

But before Wiley could finish his sentence, they all heard it.

A howl . . .

Coming from outside the tent, down a ways, and just a little behind.

Then another howl . . . and another . . . The hair rose on the back of Drake's neck. "Great Scott! We're surrounded! There's an *army* of werewolves out there!"

Suddenly, the floor of the tent began to bubble. And boil. And ripple and roil. And then, just when they thought it couldn't get any more frightening, a most horrible howl came from *beneath their feet.*

"Jeepers creepers!" screamed Wiley. "The werewolves are clawing their way through the floor!"

"Emergency evacuation procedure!" cried Drake and Nell. "No time to lose!"

Together with Wiley, they dragged Mr. Millard—sleeping bag and all—out of the tent, zipping it shut behind them.

"Stand back, everybody!" cried Nell.

Then, before their very eyes, the tent blew up like a balloon.

Bigger and bigger . . . Howling and howling . . .

Until it began to rise in the air, straining against the stakes. One by one, the stakes popped out of the ground. Then the tent floated off into the steamy night. . . .

CHAPTER THREE

Creepy Campout Analysis

"**A**mazing," said Nell.

"Fascinating," said Drake.

"Werewolves can do that?" asked Wiley.

While they watched, the tent hovered in the moonlight, eerily glowing like a ghost before slowly deflating and sinking to the ground.

"Hmm," said Drake. "Are you thinking what I'm thinking, Scientist Nell?"

"Indeed I am, Detective Doyle."

"Problem?" asked Mr. Doyle, glancing over his newspaper.

"Nothing Doyle and Fossey can't handle, Mr. Doyle," said Nell. "Kindly wake Mr. Millard while Detective Doyle and I fetch the tent. We must return to the lab for analysis."

"I'm on it," said Mr. Doyle. And he was. After all, Mr. Doyle was their man.

Back at the parking lot, Mr. Millard loaded the rest of the camping gear into his truck. "No video games for a week, Wiley."

"A week? But—but—"

"We'll buy a tent and camp again tomorrow. There are no such things as werewolves."

"But—but—" Wiley turned to Drake and Nell. "You've got to help me, *please!*"

"Not to worry," said Drake. "Whatever is happening, we'll get to the bottom of it."

So without further ado, Drake, Nell, and Mr. Doyle hopped into their car and zoomed off.

Back at the lab, Drake and Nell got to work.

Nell examined the tent. Drake pulled a book off the shelf and thumbed through until he found the right section: "Creepy Campout Analysis: What to Do When Werewolves Howl All Around You, Your Imagination Goes Bazonkers, and Your Tent Floats Off into the Night."

Just then, Mrs. Kate Doyle poked her head around the door. While Mr. Doyle was great for squealing around corners, Mrs. Doyle was fabulous for food and drink—so fabulous that she owned her own catering company. "Need anything?" she asked. "Hot chocolate, maybe?"

"No, thanks," said Drake.

"Just coffee," said Nell. "Decaf. Black."

"Affirmative," said Mrs. Doyle. And she was back in a flash with coffee. No cream, no sugar, just coffee. "I'm off to bed," she said.

"Check," they said.

Nell phoned her mother, Ann Fossey. "Campout emergency, Mom. We're pulling an all-nighter."

"Ah, yes." You see, Nell's mother knew about all-nighters. Professor Fossey taught wildlife biology at Mossy Lake University, where all-nighters were quite common. Especially when one was observing the nocturnal habits of whiskered screech owls. "Don't drink too much coffee, and call me in the morning."

"Check."

Click.

Next Drake and Nell shared their observations. Then they developed a hypothesis. (As all scientists know, a hypothesis is your best guess as to what is happening and why.) Nell said, "Based on our observations, Detective Doyle, I believe the tent floated off because . . ."

Drake listened carefully. "Agreed. Let's test our hypothesis."

So for the rest of the night, that's exactly what they did. They built simulations. They tested this. They tested that. And by the time they'd finished breakfast (strawberry crêpes, plus orange slices and hot blueberry muffins, compliments of Mrs. Doyle), Drake and Nell had their answer.

Drake phoned Wiley. "Mr. Millard? If you would be so kind as to come to the lab . . ."

"How many werewolves do I have to battle tonight?" said Wiley the moment he arrived. "A hundred? A thousand? Did you develop a secret weapon? Maybe an anti-full-moon formula?"

"First things first, Mr. Millard," said Drake. "Have a seat and allow Scientist Nell to explain."

Nell whacked the chalkboard with her long, wooden pointer. "Imagine the Earth as a peach, if you will. Have you ever eaten a peach?"

Wiley scratched his head. "Uh, do I get bonus points for this?"

"The skin of the peach is like the *crust* of the Earth. The crust is the solid outer layer on which we stand." Nell stamped the floor to demonstrate.

"Ah, yes, the crust," said Drake. "Quite solid. Rocks and whatnot."

Nell said, "Now, the juicy flesh of the peach is like the Earth's *mantle*. The mantle is hotter and softer than the crust."

"Quite so," said Drake.

"Finally," said Nell, "the pit of the peach is like the *core* of the Earth. The core is very hot."

Wiley frowned. "What I can't figure out is just *how* the werewolves floated the tent. Are werewolves allowed to have wings? 'Cause I don't think that's allowed. That's against the rules."

Nell whacked the chalkboard again with her wooden pointer. "Listen carefully, Mr. Millard. Your life may depend upon it."

Wiley gulped. "My—my *life?*"

"Affirmative," said Drake. He clasped his hands behind his back and began to pace. "Now, the core of the Earth is composed of two parts. The inner core is solid, but the outer core is composed of hot liquid rock, called *magma*."

"Also known as *lava*," said Nell.

Drake pushed up his glasses with his finger. "As you can imagine, all of the heat beneath the Earth's surface creates pressure. When a volcano erupts, the Earth is releasing this pressure."

"Quite right, Detective Doyle," said Nell. "It's like a pot of boiling water with the lid on so tightly that no steam is allowed to escape. Eventually the pressure from the steam blows the lid off."

"Now," said Wiley, "about those werewolves?"

Drake stopped his pacing and looked quite serious. "That's just it, Mr. Millard. There aren't any werewolves."

Wiley looked stunned. As if he'd just found out there were no such things as mashed potatoes, or baseball games, or arms and legs. "But—but—the howling. I heard—you both heard—"

"Indeed," said Drake. "But it wasn't werewolves making that racket—it was *steam*."

"Steam?" For a second, Wiley looked disappointed, for as everyone knows, battling steam is not nearly as exciting as battling werewolves.

"It was a *fumarole*, to be precise," said Nell.

Wiley laughed. "What the heck is that?"

"A fumarole is no laughing matter," said Nell.

"Indeed not," said Drake.

"Fumaroles are caused when water drains down into the Earth and pools next to magma," said Nell. "The water heats—"

"Steam is produced—" added Drake.

"And the pressure forces the steam out of the Earth's crust," continued Nell, "sometimes with a howl, like a boiling hot teakettle."

"What about the stinky air?" asked Wiley.

"Dissolved minerals in the steam," said Drake.

"And the tent floating off?" asked Wiley.

"Again," said Nell, "steam. When you tangled with the thorn bush, you accidentally tore a hole in the floor of the tent, allowing steam to enter. As we know, steam is very hot, and hot air rises."

Drake drew a quick diagram on the chalkboard. "Basically, your tent became a hot air balloon. We escaped just in the nick of time."

"So I pitched my tent on a fumerole?"

"Correct," said Drake. "No more camping on Waxberry Hill. We'll send a full report to your father."

Wiley shook their hands. "Amazing work. How can I thank you enough?"

"Our pleasure," said Drake and Nell.

Later, Drake wrote in his lab notebook:

Wiley one happy ~~camper~~ customer.
Park service notified about fumaroles.
Received "Warriors Versus Werewolves" video game.
Must return in one week.
          Paid in full.

CHAPTER FOUR
Picnic in Peril

It was a perfect morning in Mossy Lake for observing mama birds and their hatchlings. In fact, perched on a ladder in her backyard, Nell Fossey was doing just that. She peered between the tree branches. She adjusted her binoculars. She sketched a bird in her notebook.

And just as she was about to sigh happily, her cell phone rang.

"Doyle and Fossey," she answered.

"Thank goodness you're home," said the caller.

Nell recognized the voice. It was Mary Elizabeth Pendleton. Not only was Mary a repeat customer, but she was a proper young lady. Born with a teacup in one hand and a lace hankie in the other, she had read all the works of Shakespeare and could recite lovely sonnets. Her tea parties were simply not to be missed.

"What can I do for you, Ms. Pendleton?"

"Today I'm having my delightful picnic on the banks of Plum River."

"I hadn't forgotten. Two o'clock, was it?"

"That's what I like about you, Nell. Ever so punctual. However—" Mary paused. "I've only just arrived and—well, there's a slight situation."

"Situation?"

"I'm afraid my picnic is in peril. It—it would be ever so helpful if you and Detective Doyle could pop over for a moment. You simply must see this for yourselves."

"Check. Fifteen minutes and counting."

"Splendid. Cheerio."

Click.

Nell phoned Drake. "Mary Elizabeth Pendleton's picnic's in peril. Plum River. ASAP."

"Check."

Click.

Plum River was, well, a plum of a river. Sparkling water gurgled. Trees, shrubs, and grassy hills lined the banks, while birds flitted to and fro.

21

Nell and Drake arrived at the same time. (Not only that, but they arrived *on* time as well, as should all top-notch science detectives.) They hurried over to where Mary sat under a tree as she arranged a bouquet of flowers just so.

"Doyle and Fossey, at your service," said Nell.

"Good day, Ms. Pendleton," said Drake, shaking Mary's hand.

"So good of you to come," Mary replied.

Nell whipped out her notebook and pencil. "Now, what seems to be the trouble?"

"As I always say, a picture's worth a thousand words." Mary led the way across the grass, down a little embankment, and to the river.

When Drake and Nell saw the river, they gasped in horror.

"Egads!" cried Drake.

"Oh, no!" cried Nell.

Mary shook her head sadly. "Quite tragic."

Yes, quite tragic indeed. For washed up on the banks of the river lay dozens, maybe hundreds, of fish—*all dead*.

"This is an ecological catastrophe," said Nell, feeling a bit weak in the knees, as if she'd just lost dozens of her best friends, which, scientifically speaking, she had.

"But—but—" Drake scratched his head, puzzled. "How—why?"

"I have no idea. That's why I've hired the two of you," said Mary. "A picnic is no picnic with such tragedy in the air. Perhaps there's something you can do to help. I'd hate to reschedule."

"You can count on us," said Drake.

Mary checked her watch. "Only three hours until everyone arrives for the picnic."

"We'll get to work immediately," said Nell.

So, while Mary went back to her flower arranging, Drake and Nell whipped out their waterproof periscopes and their specimen jars. They pulled on their surgical gloves. *Snap!*

First they took samples of the water. Then they put some dead fish in sturdy plastic bags for analysis. Then they hiked upriver, searching for more clues.

Soon they came to Badger Creek, which emptied into Plum River. Drake took another water sample, dating and labeling the specimen jar BADGER CREEK. He peered at the sample. "Looks normal," he observed.

At that moment, a breeze blew, and on the breeze was a nasty smell.

"Do you smell that?" asked Nell.

"It appears to be coming from somewhere over there." Drake pointed up Badger Creek to a chain-link fence. A sign said: PRIVATE PROPERTY: KEEP OUT! The creek meandered under the fence and disappeared into the woods beyond. "Hmm," said Drake. "Wonder what's back there." They walked to the fence and peered through their binoculars into the woods.

"Don't know," said Nell. "Whatever it is, it sure is stinky. Well, Detective Doyle, stinky or not, we must hike up Plum River and continue our investigation. Shall we?"

So they jumped from rock to rock across Badger Creek and continued to hike up Plum River. They hadn't gone very far when Nell saw something amazing. Something remarkable. Something so unexpected, she stopped in her tracks.

"What is it?" asked Drake, bumping into her back and hurting his nose with an *oof!* and an *ow!* "More dead fish?"

Nell stuck her periscope underwater and peered through it. "Quite the opposite, Detective Doyle. See for yourself."

Drake peered through the periscope. "Great Scott, Naturalist Nell! The fish are swimming along, happy as can be! And I can't see any dead fish! This is amazing. This is remarkable. This is so unexpected. What do you think it means?"

"I'm not sure, but I have my suspicions."

"Likewise," said Drake.

Nell took another water sample, dating and labeling it PLUM RIVER, UPRIVER FROM BADGER CREEK. FISH ALIVE. "If our suspicions are correct, we've no time to lose. Hundreds, if not thousands, of lives are at stake." She removed her gloves with a *snap!*

"Right as rain, Naturalist Nell. To Nature Headquarters we go! Doyle and Fossey to the rescue!"

CHAPTER FIVE

A Terrible Answer

Nature Headquarters was the code name for Nell's bedroom. Truth be told, it looked more like a jungle than a bedroom. Papier-mâché trees soared, covered with sparkly leaves and vines. Everywhere there were terrariums, aquariums, and cages filled with snakes, turtles, mice, ants, and, oh, too many other creatures for the average person to name and count (although Nell knew and loved them all).

Drake and Nell hurried into Nature Head-quarters. Drake's glasses steamed in the moist air. For a second he was a bit blinded. "Yoo-hoo, Naturalist Nell," he cried, relieved when he felt a hand on his arm steering him to the chair at the desk. Then, like all top-notch scientific teams who have a job to do, Drake and Nell got to work. First they discussed their observations. Then they formed a hypothesis. Nell said, "I believe what's happening to the fish at Plum River is . . ."

Drake listened, then nodded. "Agreed. Let's get busy, shall we?"

So they did.

Nell pulled on her surgical gloves. *Snap!* She poured. She measured. She analyzed. She said, "Hmm" and "Aha!" And if that weren't enough, she also drew graphs and charts.

Meanwhile, Drake browsed the Internet. He read newspaper articles. He zoomed in on satellite images. He said, "Hmm" and "I wonder . . ." and "Gadzooks!"

At 12:31, they ate lunch. (Once they explained that they were under a deadline and that hundreds, if not thousands, of fish lives were at stake, Professor Fossey was kind enough to fix PB&Js, with sliced peaches for dessert.)

Finally, after they'd finished testing and zooming and eating, Drake and Nell had their answer. A terrible answer, but an answer nonetheless.

Nell called Mary. "Ms. Pendleton? We'll be there in fifteen minutes to explain everything. Meanwhile, pack up your picnic."

Mary gasped. "Pack up my . . . oh dear, I must say, I was afraid it would come to this. Dead fish are just so . . . so *improper*. But, whatever you say, Nell. You're the professional. Cheerio."

Fourteen minutes and one second later, Drake and Nell were once again at Plum River. Mary sat on her blanket, her picnic baskets all neatly packed. She dabbed her eyes with a hankie. "I suppose I'll need to call everyone to cancel the picnic."

Drake checked his watch. "That would be most premature, Ms. Pendleton."

Mary looked confused. "But—but—you told me to pack . . ."

"Indeed we did," said Drake. "Naturalist Nell?"

"Thank you, Detective Doyle." Nell looked quite serious, as top-notch scientists often do. She began to pace. "You see, Ms. Pendleton, it was clear that *something* in Plum River was killing the fish—but what? And where was it coming from? Badger Creek gave us our first clue."

"But what on *earth* does Badger Creek have to do with Plum River?" asked Mary.

"Everything, as it turns out," replied Nell. "You see, Badger Creek empties into Plum River."

"Of course," said Mary. "Everyone knows that."

"Downriver from Badger Creek," continued Nell, "the fish were all dead, as you well know. But *upriver* from the creek, the fish were all alive, meaning that whatever was killing the fish was coming from Badger Creek."

"So when we returned to Nature Headquarters," Drake said, "Naturalist Nell tested the pH in the water samples we had collected."

"Whatever do you mean?" Mary asked. "What is pH?"

"Ah, so glad you asked," said Drake, pushing up his glasses with his finger. "Very simply, pH is a scale that tells you whether something is an acid, a base, or neutral. Tell me, Ms. Pendleton, have you ever taken a spoonful of vinegar?"

Mary shuddered. "Oh my, yes."

"Vinegar is a type of acid," said Drake. "So is lemon juice. Quite puckery. Now, tell me, have you ever nibbled on a piece of chalk? Not that I recommend it, mind you."

"Oh my, no," said Mary. "How uncivilized."

"Chalk is a type of base, as is soap," Drake explained. "Acids and bases are opposites."

"Finally," added Nell, "there are neutrals. Pure water is neutral, meaning it is neither an acid nor a base, but is in between. Most rivers that fish inhabit are neutral. Knowing this, I tested the pH levels in our three water samples—"

"While I," said Drake, "using the latest in satellite technology, explored Badger Creek on the Internet. What we discovered was quite disturbing."

"Disturbing?" asked Mary.

"About one mile up Badger Creek," explained Drake, "is an industrial plant. I zoomed in on it with a satellite and observed that one of their tanks was leaking. Very simply, the runoff was emptying into Badger Creek and polluting the water."

"I confirmed this with my pH tests," said Nell. "Although the Badger Creek water looked quite normal, it was acidic. This acidic pollution poured out of Badger Creek into Plum River, killing all the fish downstream. Indeed, the water downstream tested acidic, while the water upstream from Badger Creek was neutral, as it should be."

Mary sniffed and dabbed her eyes with her hankie. "So tragic. I don't suppose a picnic matters much when so many fish have perished."

Drake patted her shoulder. "Cheer up, Ms. Pendleton. All is not lost."

"Detective Doyle is right," said Nell. "We'll

help you move your picnic upriver to where the fish are still quite happy."

"You—you will?" asked Mary.

"And," added Drake, "we'll post signs directing everyone to your new location."

Mary brightened. "Oh, you are ever so splendid! But—but—there is one thing that still troubles me. What about all the fish upriver, who are, even now, swimming to their deaths?"

"Ah," said Nell. "We've already alerted the authorities. They'll investigate immediately. No doubt, the factory will have to clean up its act and pay a huge fine, as it should."

Mary gave them each a hug. "Job well done! Jolly good!"

"Our pleasure," said Nell, handing her a business card.

That evening, Nell e-mailed Drake:

```
Pollution no picnic.
Authorities say cleaning the river
is their number one priority.
Received two tickets to the Mossy
Lake Aquarium.
Professor Fossey says "Bravo!"
--Naturalist Nell
```

CHAPTER SIX
Paleo Pals Club

Drake put on his headset.

He flipped the switch . . . *beep*.

He pressed the button . . . *boop*.

He whirled this knob . . . *bing* . . . and dialed that knob . . . *boing*.

"Earth to outer space," Drake said into the microphone. "Earth to outer space. Anyone read me? Hello, Martians?" *Beep. Beep.* "Plutonians?" *Boop. Boop.* "Proxima Centaurians?" *Bing. Bing. Boing. Boing.* "Drake Doyle here . . . come in, come in."

Suddenly Drake heard a scratch. Then a muffled *woof*.

"Great Scott! I hear you, I hear you! Can you bark a little louder?"

WOOF!

"Louder, please!"

WOOF! WOOF!

"Goodness!" cried Drake, quite excited. "If I didn't know better, I'd say you were sitting right next to me!"

Just then he felt a bit of slobber slide across his knee. He gave a little shriek (a most unscientific shriek) before realizing his error. "Oh, it's you. Hello, Dr. Livingston."

After patting Dr. Livingston's head and telling him he was a good boy, Drake turned his radio off. (Communicating with space aliens would have to wait for another day. Nell sent Dr. Livingston only when there was an important matter at hand.)

"What do you have for me today?" Drake reached into the dog's pouch and pulled out a piece of paper that began:

—··/··/—··//—·——/———/···//··—·/———/·—·/——·/·/—///

Now, to the untrained eye, it might look like a chicken had tripped across the paper. But Drake knew better. He put his superior decoding skills to work. Finally the note looked less like chicken scratch and more like a secret message. It read:

Did you forget?
Contest today for best fossil.
Pepper Stonewright the sure winner.
Meet me at Paleo Pals Club ASAP.
—Scientist Nell

"Egads! How could I have forgotten? Nell's covering the contest for our weekly newsletter, *Amazing Science for Geniuses and the Merely Curious*. Come, Dr. Livingston!" Drake fetched his detective kit and hurried down the attic stairs. "To the Paleo Pals Club we go!"

Woof! Woof!

The Paleo Pals Club was the perfect sort of club if you loved fossils or simply liked to dig in the dirt. Every year, the Paleo Pals Club held a contest, offering a prize for the best fossil. What was the prize? An all-expenses-paid trip to the Buzzard Badlands, where folks have been known to trip over fossilized dinosaur bones. Plus a feature article in *Junior Paleo Pals Geographic*. All very exciting, really.

Drake parked his bike and hurried inside with Dr. Livingston. (Normally, Drake wouldn't dare take Dr. Livingston anywhere near a pile of bones, but in this case the bones were hard as rocks and not very tasty.)

"Ah, there you are." Nell had a camera around her neck and a pencil behind her ear. She looked quite reporter-like. "I was beginning to worry."

"My apologies, Scientist Nell. Communications with Martians, you know."

"Understood. Let me show you around."

Nell took Drake on a little tour. There were posters and colorful streamers and plenty of punch and cookies for everyone. Of course, there were all kinds of fossils, too—teeth, turtles, trilobites, and the like. A judge moved among the display tables as he scribbled on his clipboard.

Pepper Stonewright, the president of the Paleo Pals Club, waved them over to her table. "It's a trilobite," she explained, as Drake examined her fossil with his magnifying glass. "Trilobites were sea creatures that lived 250 to 520 million years ago."

"Lovely," he said. "Rather looks like a giant bug."

Woof! said Dr. Livingston, giving the trilobite a sniff.

Pepper sighed happily. "It's the largest, most complete fossil I've ever found. As you probably know, we're required to have found the fossil ourselves. Not only that, but we must disclose the location of our dig. You know—tell everyone where we found it."

"Fascinating," said Nell.

"Plus we have to make a site map."

"Let me guess," said Drake. "A site map details where every fossil was found."

"Right," said Pepper. "It's pretty easy if it's a trilobite. Not so easy if, let's say, it's a dinosaur with lots of bones scattered about."

Nell jotted in her notebook. "You sound quite experienced, Ms. Stonewright. Tell me, how long have you been fossil hunting?"

"Ever since I could crawl. I'm going to be a paleontologist when I grow up."

"A worthy career," said Drake.

"Winning this prize would mean the world to me. I've dreamed of going to the Buzzard Badlands for as long as I can remember. And—" Pepper lowered her voice to a whisper. "Judging by the other fossils, I think I'll snag that prize."

"Anything you'd like our readers to know?" Nell said, scribbling in her notebook.

"Fossils rock!" said Pepper. Then she smiled and posed for the camera. *Flash!*

"Good luck, Ms. Stonewright," said Nell, shaking her hand. "And thank you for the excellent information. Our readers will be delighted."

"My pleasure."

Just then, there was a commotion over in the corner. A crowd had gathered.

"What's going on over there?" Drake asked.

"Don't know," said Pepper. "That's James Frisco's table. He's late again—"

"*Frisco!*" Drake and Nell gasped, exchanging horrified glances.

Woof! Woof! cried Dr. Livingston.

"He's our newest member," Pepper was saying. "He's got a lot to learn, though. Don't think he knows a fossil from a rock."

"Whatever he's up to," Drake said to Nell, "it can't be good."

"Agreed," said Nell. "Let's go investigate."

So, along with Pepper and Dr. Livingston, they hurried over to join the crowd.

Sure enough, it was Frisco. A curtain was behind him. A table was in front of him. On the table was a cloth. And under the cloth was something lumpy . . .

"Without further ado," Frisco was saying, "I shall unveil my amazing fossil. Stand back, everyone, because it doesn't get any better than this!" So saying, Frisco whipped the cloth away.

There, for all the Paleo Pals Club members to see, was an animal track (a fossilized *cast*, in paleo terms). But not just any animal track. No, indeed.

"This," declared Frisco, "is the fossilized footprint of a T. rex!"

"Oooh! Aaah!" cried the crowd.

It was really quite stunning.

"Did I just say that it doesn't get any better?" asked Frisco. "Well, ha ha! I lied! Because where there's a footprint, there's the creature that made the footprint! Behold . . . the one and only . . . the best, the most fabulous and horrifying . . . ha ha! . . . BEAST!" And he whipped the curtain open.

"Oh my gosh!" cried Nell, her jaw dropping.

"Great Scott!" cried Drake, his knees turning to jelly.

Woof! Woof! cried Dr. Livingston, who hid behind Nell.

"Eek!" cried the crowd.

"I can't believe it!" cried Pepper. *"It's a T. rex!"*

CHAPTER SEVEN
Dino-Disaster

It was awesome. It was fearsome.

It made the fossilized animal track look like mouse doo-doo. (Never before in the history of Mossy Lake had anyone found so much as a dinosaur bone, much less an entire T. rex skeleton.)

Once the crowd realized that they were in no real danger of being gobbled up, they went wild. They circled around, pointing and exclaiming. Cell phones went *beep* and *boop*.

The judge proclaimed, "Well, I think we all know who the winner will be . . . but according to the contest rules, I can't declare Frisco—uh, I mean, the winner—until three o'clock."

"Not to worry," said Frisco, waving to the flashing cameras. "Everyone knows I'm the sure winner. Nothing to it, really. Just cleverness and brilliance, as usual."

"No doubt congratulations will be in order," said Pepper, shaking Frisco's hand. "Anyone who finds a T. rex fossil deserves to win."

"Gee, thanks, President Pepper," said Frisco, with a smirk. "I'll remember your kind words while I'm digging up dinosaur bones in the Badlands and having my photo taken for the cover of the magazine. Better luck next year."

Meanwhile, Drake, Nell, and Dr. Livingston were studying the T. rex. Drake was drawing a sketch in his notebook. Nell was taking photos. Dr. Livingston was sniffing around.

"Do you see what I see?" asked Drake.

"Indeed I do, Detective Doyle," said Nell.

Flash! Flash!

"Something foul is afoot," said Drake.

"Something foul indeed," said Nell.

Sniff, sniff, grr, said Dr. Livingston.

Just then, Frisco walked up. "What are you two geek brains looking at? Show's over, so you can get lost now. And your little dog, too."

"Actually," said Nell, smiling brightly, "getting lost sounds like a great idea right about now."

Frisco looked startled. "It does? I mean, yeah,

it does. So, what are you waiting for?" He turned to face the crowd. "Ah—my adoring fans . . ."

"I'm assuming you have a brilliant plan?" Drake asked Nell. (You see, Nell didn't normally get lost, so if she *wanted* to get lost, she had to have a plan.) Nell lowered her voice. "Remember what Pepper told us? That everybody has to submit the location of their dig, plus a site map?"

Drake nodded.

"Frisco's site maps are on his table. What do you say we grab one and pay a visit to the site?"

"Good thinking," said Drake. "We'll see what we can dig up."

Nell glanced over at Pepper, who stood off to the side looking quite forlorn. "It's the least we can do for Pepper."

Drake checked his watch. "The judging is in two hours. There's no time to lose!"

First, Drake and Nell stopped by the lab to fetch supplies. Then they were off on their bicycles, while Dr. Livingston ran alongside.

When they arrived at the dig site, the air was hot and dusty. Overhead, an eagle screeched. And under the shadow of a rock, a lizard slithered. A sign read:

FRISCO'S FABULOUS DINOSAUR SITE
I SAW IT FIRST.
GET LOST!

"Let's get to work, shall we?" said Drake.

"Check," said Nell.

Woof! said Dr. Livingston.

For the next hour, they investigated. They dug. They sifted. They took samples. They surveyed. Nell snapped photos. Drake drew diagrams. And Dr. Livingston snoozed in the shade. Then, after a two-and-a-half-minute lunch where the view just didn't get any better, they returned to the lab for analysis.

Nell found a book on the shelf and turned to the page titled "Dinosaur Dilemma: What to Do When the Crowd Goes Wild, Something Foul Is Afoot, and a T. rex Stomps on Your Trilobite." She read the section aloud, then said, "Let's share our observations."

By the time they'd formed and tested their hypothesis, it was five minutes to three.

"We have our answer!" cried Drake.

"To the Paleo Pals Club we go!" cried Nell.

Woof! Woof! cried Dr. Livingston.

They hopped on their bicycles and pedaled like mad to the Paleo Pals Club. (All of this pedaling-like-mad stuff was really very good exercise. Drake was feeling quite energized. Except, sadly, when he hit a pothole and fell, *splat!* Nothing too energizing about that.) Drake and Nell arrived just as the judge faced the crowd.

"Well," the judge was saying, "this year, I must say, you've exceeded all our expectations. Especially Frisco. I mean, wow. That's why it should come as no surprise that Frisco's the win—"

"Stop everything!" cried Drake and Nell, hurrying to the front of the crowd.

The judge frowned. "This is most irregular."

Frisco tapped his watch. "Uh—time? Hello? Don't you lab rats ever use a watch? It's time for the prize giveaway."

"Allow us to explain," said Drake, a bit out of breath.

Nell added, "We have vital information that could change the outcome of the contest."

The crowd gasped.

Frisco rolled his eyes. "Spare me."

The judge checked his watch. "Make it fast."

Drake faced the crowd and pushed up his glasses with his finger. "We first became suspicious when we noticed that the T. rex fossil was *too* perfect."

"Hey," said Frisco. "Perfection is my middle name."

"As you know," Nell said, ignoring Frisco, "most fossils are in terrible shape. Some fossils require *years* of expert restoration."

Frisco yawned. "And your point is?"

"Second," continued Drake, "there was an extra bone in the spine, a bone commonly known as a vertebra."

Frisco frowned. "Really? Uh—I mean, yeah. Heh heh. Did that on purpose. Just to see if any of you losers were paying attention."

"An extra vertebra in the spine, you say?" The judge scribbled on his clipboard.

"Indeed," said Nell. She began to pace, her hands clasped behind her back. Drake could tell she was quite serious. "After we realized that the T. rex had an extra vertebra, we paid a visit to the dig site. Now, as many of you are aware, the crust of the Earth's surface is made up of layers of dirt and rock, all piled on top of one another."

"News to me," said Frisco.

"Case in point," said Drake, "the walls of the Grand Canyon. You can see the dirt and rock in various layers."

"Excellent example, Detective Doyle," said

Nell. "The oldest layer is on the bottom, while the newest layer is on the top."

Pepper gasped. "I remember studying that in school! It's called *stratification*."

"Correct," said Nell with a nod. "Likewise, fossils will also be found in layers, according to when the animal was alive."

"For instance, Ms. Stonewright," said Drake, "you told us that your trilobite fossil is about 250 to 520 million years old. That means you can find trilobite fossils only in layers of Earth that are also 250 to 520 million years old."

"Sounds right to me," said Pepper.

"Sounds stupid to me," said Frisco.

"But what if," suggested Nell, "someone 'found' a trilobite fossil in dirt that was only 100 million years old—"

Pepper thought hard. Then she said, "It would be a *fake*!"

"Fake, schmake," mumbled Frisco.

"Precisely, Ms. Stonewright," said Nell. "Because 100 million years ago, trilobites had already been extinct for some 150 million years."

The judge frowned. "Hmm . . . I'm not sure where this is headed, and time is ticking. . . ."

"Then let's make this simple," said Nell. She

stopped pacing and faced the crowd. "The dirt and rocks at Frisco's dig site are approximately 5 million years old—"

"But," continued Drake, "dinosaurs became extinct approximately 65 million years ago, meaning the T. rex fossil is a . . . is a . . ."

Just then, something astonishing happened. Something quite extraordinary. You see, a little breeze blew through the room. And with the breeze, the T. rex trembled. It wobbled. It creaked.

And then, as everyone watched, the T. rex broke apart and fell on the floor with a *CRASH!* and a *CLATTER!*

The dust settled.

The crowd gasped.

The judge dropped his clipboard.

Because, you see, there, scattered across the floor for everyone to see, was a mess of plaster and chicken wire. Hardly the stuff fossils are made of.

"Aha!" cried Drake.

"Case closed!" cried Nell.

Woof! cried Dr. Livingston.

"My dinosaur!" cried Frisco.

"It's a FAKE!" roared the crowd.

The judge picked up his clipboard. "Like I said, *most* irregular!" He then cleared his throat and pronounced, "Well, ahem, seeing as the T. rex isn't really a T. rex at all, I declare this year's winner to be Pepper Stonewright! Congratulations, Pepper! Excellent trilobite!"

Pepper went up to receive the grand prize.

Nell told her to say, "Trilobites love cheese!"

Flash! Flash!

"Thank you, Drake and Nell," said Pepper afterward, shaking their hands. "I never would have won if it hadn't been for you. You rock."

"Our pleasure," said Nell.

"All in a day's work," said Drake, handing Pepper their business card. "Call us. Anytime."

Later, Drake wrote in his lab notebook:

Case of the terrible T. rex solved.
Frisco a fraud.
Newsletter selling like hotcakes.
Pepper says she'll bring us a fossil
from the badlands. (Triceratops,
perhaps?)
Satisfaction complete.

CHAPTER EIGHT

Crispy Critters

It was late on a Sunday afternoon when Drake returned home. He'd just spent the weekend at the beach with his parents and was rather pooped. But before he could put away his mask and fins and hang his polka-dot swim trunks up to dry, the phone rang.

"Doyle and Fossey," Drake answered.

"*¿Hola?* Is this Drake Doyle?"

Drake recognized the caller. It was Rosa Alvarez from class. Now, Rosa was a cheerful sort, famous for her fine fiestas where there was plenty of cheer for everyone—piñatas, tacos, music, and swimming in the pool. (Just last week Drake had attended a fiesta and had felt quite cheered.)

Drake sat at his desk and whipped a pencil out

from behind his ear. (You see, amateur science detective geniuses must always be prepared. Snorkeling with a pencil behind your ear is challenging, but not impossible.) "Ah, Ms. Alvarez, *hola, hola.* What can I do for you?"

"I—I need your help. I'm trying to bake a *tres leche* cake. A three-milk cake—my mother's favorite. You see, it's my mother's birthday and I'm throwing a surprise fiesta for her tonight."

"Ah, a happy birthday to her." Drake wrote in his notebook: *Rosa bakes delicious cake.*

"*Gracias.* But everything has gone wrong. The first time I made the cake, it didn't come out right. It was raw in the middle and overcooked on the bottom. So I tried again, and the same thing happened. So now I try again. For the third time."

"Let me guess. The cake is still raw?"

"No, I—I mean, *sí,* it's still raw. What I mean is, I haven't started to bake it yet. Because my oven . . . well, it . . ." Rosa paused. "What I am trying to tell you, *Señor* Doyle, is that . . . my oven, well . . ." Rosa's voice dropped to a whisper. "It is acting strangely."

"Acting strangely?"

"*Sí.* When I opened the oven door, it . . . it *spoke to me.*"

"It *spoke* to you?" asked Drake, rather alarmed. "What did it say?"

"'You're next, little lady.'"

Drake gasped, his scientific mind whirling. Could it be? Rosa was in the hands of a . . . of a *loco* oven! Or . . . or maybe it was a transforming robot, only *disguised* as an oven! Maybe in another minute or so it would transform into a terrifying robot and cook Rosa to a crisp!

"Please, *Señor* Doyle," Rosa was saying, "you must help me! I am running out of time! My mother will be so disappointed if there is no cake!"

"Say no more. Doyle and Fossey will take the case. Meanwhile, arm yourself with a spatula. We'll be there in eight minutes, tops."

Immediately Drake phoned Nell. "Rosa requires rescue from robot. No time to lose. Eight minutes, tops."

"Check."

Click.

Seven minutes and fifty-seven seconds later, Drake arrived. Nell was already waiting on Rosa's front porch.

"Detective Doyle," said Nell with a nod.

"Scientist Nell," said Drake, nodding in return.

Just then, Rosa opened the door. (Sad to say, her usual smile was turned upside down. Rather like a droopy flower without any water at all.) "*Hola, mis amigos. Gracias* for coming."

"Doyle and Fossey at your service," said Drake. "Now, if you would be so kind as to lead us to the robot . . . I—I mean to the oven in question."

While Rosa led the way to the kitchen, Drake filled Nell in on the details of the case. Nell whispered, "Sounds serious indeed. If we're not careful, we could all be crispy critters."

Once in the kitchen, Drake and Nell got to work. "Stand back, Ms. Alvarez," Drake cautioned. The two scientists put on their protective goggles and observed the oven.

"Oven appears normal," whispered Nell.

"Appearances can be deceiving when dealing with transforming robots," whispered Drake. "If it starts to transform, we must evacuate immediately."

"Understood."

"Readout indicates a temperature of 350 degrees Fahrenheit," observed Drake. "Quite normal for baking a cake."

"Oven is electric, not gas," noted Nell. She

flipped on the oven light and peered through the glass door. "There are two heating elements—one on the top and one on the bottom."

Drake turned to Rosa. "Tell me, Ms. Alvarez. How long have you owned this oven?"

"Five years or so. Since we first moved here."

Drake and Nell exchanged glances.

"It appears to be a very patient robot," Drake said to Nell. "Perhaps it was waiting for orders from the mother ship."

Nell nodded. "So, Detective Doyle, now that we have completed our external observations, shall we open the oven?"

"We shall," said Drake.

Both Drake and Nell slipped on oven mitts. Drake took a deep breath. Nell took a deep breath. Then, carefully, very carefully indeed, Drake and Nell opened the oven door. . . .

But instead of talking, instead of transforming into a terrifying robot, the oven was silent. In fact, it looked and sounded very much like an oven should look and sound. Very ovenlike.

"Are you certain you heard it talk, Ms. Alvarez?" asked Nell, peering into the oven.

"*Sí.*"

"Uh—did you know one of your elements is broken?" said Drake. Indeed, the bottom element now glowed orange-hot, while the upper element remained cold and dark.

Rosa frowned. "But it worked fine yesterday."

"Likely that is why your cakes did not bake correctly," said Nell, scribbling in her lab notebook.

"Agreed," said Drake. He stood, adjusting his goggles with his oven mitt. "Well, I guess you must have been hearing things, Ms. Alvarez. Likely the heat. Hot day, hot oven, you know—"

Just then, like a sleeping giant that suddenly awakens, the oven spoke. "Oh boy, ha ha ha! You said that right! *Ha ha ha ha ha!*"

CHAPTER NINE

Fiesta Fiasco

"**E**gads!" cried Drake, stumbling into the cupboards.

"Oh my gosh!" cried Nell, dropping her pencil into the cake batter.

"*¡Ay, caramba!*" cried Rosa, waving her spatula in front of her.

"Ha ha ha!" laughed the oven. "Yup, this heat could melt a turnip! Hotter 'n blue blazes! Ha ha ha—"

"Quick!" cried Drake, his lab coat caught on a cupboard knob. "Slam the oven door shut before it transforms!"

"Check!" cried Nell.

"This is KA7—" *SLAM!*

Once again, the oven was silent.

"You see?" whispered Rosa. "My oven, it is *loco*."

"*Loco* indeed," said Drake while Nell helped to untangle his lab coat from the cupboard knob.

Untangled at last, Drake thanked Nell and straightened his lab coat. "Did you hear what it said, Scientist Nell?"

"Affirmative. KA7 must be its code name. I would jot the code name into my lab notebook, except—" Nell peered at the cake batter. "I seem to have dropped my pencil."

After asking Rosa to list the ingredients in a *tres leche* cake, Drake and Nell stepped outside to look for additional clues. Drake jotted his observations in his lab notebook:

Fruit tree in front yard.
Ice cream truck—music in the air.
Giant antenna down the street.

"Hmm," said Drake. "I don't remember seeing that antenna last week at the fiesta."

"*Sí*—that's because our neighbor just put it up a couple of days ago."

"A new antenna . . ." mused Drake. He cocked his eyebrow and glanced at Nell. "Are you thinking what I'm thinking, Scientist Nell?"

"Quite possibly, Detective Doyle. But there's only one way to find out."

"Back to the lab!" cried Drake. "For analysis!"

"Expect our report ASAP, Ms. Alvarez," said Nell as she climbed on her bike.

"Meanwhile," said Drake, climbing on his bike as well, "stay out of the kitchen."

Rosa waved good-bye with her spatula. "Hurry! The guests arrive in two hours! We must have cake!"

Back at the lab, Drake and Nell wasted no time. They pulled a book off the shelf and turned to the correct section: "Loco Oven Analysis: What to Do When Your Oven Has a Code Name, Laughs Like the Dickens, and Your Fiesta Becomes a Fiasco."

After Nell read the section aloud, Drake formulated a hypothesis. He said, "I believe what's happening to Rosa's oven is . . ."

Nell listened and nodded. "Agreed. Let's test our hypothesis. Meanwhile, maybe we could ask for your mother's help."

So, with Mrs. Doyle on board (she'd said, "*No problemo*" when asked for her help), Drake and Nell tested their hypothesis. They plugged this into that. They dialed this knob. They twirled that dial.

Then they headed back to Rosa's neighborhood and conducted a quick stakeout. It took only 2.5 minutes of standing outside the neighbor's window before they had their answer. And not just any answer. The right answer.

Analysis complete, Drake and Nell hurried back to Rosa's. "We've solved the mystery, Ms. Alvarez," said Drake, as they entered the kitchen.

"But what about my cake?" Rosa asked. "Everyone will be coming soon for the surprise. There's not enough time now to bake a cake."

"First things first," said Drake. "Scientist Nell?"

"Thank you, Detective Doyle." Nell began to pace. "Are you aware, Ms. Alvarez, that there are radio waves everywhere? For instance, there are radio waves bouncing off this cake batter, off my arm, through the air, and even through outer space."

Rosa looked puzzled. "If that is true, then why can't we hear them?"

"Excellent question," said Nell. "In order to hear speech or music across radio waves, two things must occur. Detective Doyle?"

"Ah, yes, two things." Drake pushed his glasses up with his finger. "First, someone must *transmit* the speech or music. Second, someone must be able to *receive* the transmission. There is speech and music being transmitted all the time through radio waves. But you can't hear anything unless you *receive* it. Case in point—" Drake walked over to a radio sitting on the counter and flipped it on.

♪ "... *para bailar la bamba* ..." ♪

"Ah, one of my favorites." Drake tapped his foot. "You see, Ms. Alvarez, your radio is a receiver, enabling us to hear the transmission."

"Now, all of this brings up an important question." Nell stopped pacing, her hands clasped behind her back. "Why don't we hear all the radio stations at once? With all the voices and all the music in one big jumble?"

"Excellent question, Scientist Nell," Drake answered. "Because radio operators transmit on a certain *frequency*. When you turn the knob on a radio, you are dialing in different frequencies." Drake twirled the dial of the radio, and as he did, the radio stations changed.

"There are thousands of frequencies," said Nell, "all with different-size wavelengths."

"But," said Rosa, glancing at her watch, "my mother . . . the cake . . . the fiesta . . . and what does any of this have to do with my oven?"

"Ah," said Drake. "Now we come to the heart of the matter. You see, in order for something to receive a particular radio transmission, it must first be *resonant on that frequency*. Let's say there are A to Z frequencies. If someone transmits on H frequency, we must tune into H frequency in order to hear him or her. Now, we noted that your oven had one element that was broken—"

"And one that was not," said Nell. "Very simply, the two elements canceled each other out. In doing so, they created resonance on a particular radio frequency."

"Plus," added Drake, "the oven acted as a nice speaker box. Quite handy, really."

"So we were hearing a radio?" asked Rosa.

"Not just any radio," replied Nell, "but a ham radio. Your neighbor's ham radio, to be precise. His signal was very strong because he was transmitting from just down the street."

"You see, Ms. Alvarez," said Drake, "ham radio operators are amateur radio buffs. They transmit and receive radio signals from all over the world. We suspected there was a ham radio operator because of the size of the antenna. To confirm our suspicions, we listened outside your neighbor's window."

"Sure enough," said Nell. "His was the same voice we heard coming through the oven—"

"Same laugh," added Drake.

"With the same call sign beginning with KA7," said Nell. "A simple case, really."

"A piece of cake, as they say," said Drake.

"But," said Rosa, "what about when the oven said, 'You're next, little lady'?"

"Just his granddaughter, taking her turn at the radio," answered Nell.

"Our recommendation?" said Drake. "Fix the oven element. Should take care of the problem."

"Well, *gracias.*" Rosa sighed, her smile still, sadly, a little droopy. "I just wish I'd had time to bake a *tres leche* cake. Now it is too late, and everyone is due in ten minutes."

Drake cocked an eyebrow. "Ten minutes, you say? Then there's no time to lose." He whipped out a walkie-talkie from his lab-coat pocket. "Calling FF, calling FF, this is Muffin Man, over."

"You see, Ms. Alvarez," explained Nell, "a walkie-talkie is a two-way radio. It can transmit as well as receive."

The walkie-talkie crackled to life. It was Kate Doyle's voice. "Fab Foods here. Is it time?"

"Affirmative," replied Drake. "Over and out."

Five seconds later, the doorbell rang.

It was Mrs. Doyle. "Yoo-hoo! *¡Hola!* Fab Foods calling with a *tres leche* cake and decorations for a fine fiesta!"

At that very instant, a scientific miracle occurred. Rosa Alvarez's smile turned right side up. "You have saved the day!" she cried, suddenly looking quite cheery.

And as Mrs. Doyle bustled into the kitchen, Rosa turned to Drake and Nell. *"¡Gracias, mis amigos!* How can I ever repay you?"

"A piece of cake, perhaps?" said Drake.

Nell nodded. "A piece of cake, indeed."

That night, Drake wrote in his lab notebook:

Case of the loco oven solved.
Broken oven + ham radio
transmissions = talking oven.
Fiesta a smashing success.
Danced the salsa and ate tres leche
cake until I achieved maximum
capacity.

Paid in full.

Activities and Experiments for Super-Scientists

Contents

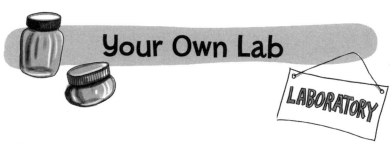

Your Own Lab

One day while hiking, you stumble across a suspiciously dirty stream. Your mission? Record your observations and collect some water samples for analysis. You reach for your specimen jars, only to realize you don't have any! Nor do you have a lab notebook! Or a lab, for that matter! Horrors! Next time, be prepared. Here's how:

1. Set up a card table and chair in your basement, your attic, or your bedroom—wherever there's room. Hang up a sign that reads LABORATORY.

2. Stock your lab with odds and ends—clean jars with lids, tape, string, fishing line, batteries, wire, funnels, clean paintbrushes—anything you think might come in handy.

3. Of course, every top-notch scientist must wear a lab coat. A white button-down shirt is perfect (ask first!). Using a permanent marker, write your name on the shirt.

4. Lastly, where would you be without a lab notebook to scribble in? Spiral or bound notebooks work great. Sharpen your pencil, write your name in your notebook, and *voila*! You can now investigate that stream!

A good lab notebook contains:
1) Experiment title
2) Method (what you plan to do)
3) Hypothesis (what you think will happen)
4) Procedure (what you did)
5) Observations (what you saw)
6) Results (what actually happened)

Good Science Tip:
Whenever you collect a water sample from your local stream, river, or lake, label the sample container with the location, date, and time. Then, in your notebook, record any observations. For example, what color is the water? Are there any odors? Is the bank muddy, rocky, or sandy? Are there plants? Are there any pipes nearby? Cover and store your sample in the refrigerator and test within twenty-four hours.

Science by the Book

While there's no single book that gives all of the answers to every science mystery (except for Drake's book, of course!), scientists are still on the same page when it comes to the **scientific method.**

Step one: scientists **observe.** They examine, they prod, they peer, and they poke. They write it all down in their lab notebooks.

Step two: based on their observations, scientists develop a **hypothesis**, which, if you recall, is a scientist's best guess as to what is really happening or what will happen. Remember Drake and Nell and the floating tent? Likely Nell's hypothesis sounded something like this: "Based on our observations, I believe the tent floated off because it was pitched over a fumarole. I believe the fumarole filled the tent with hot air, making it behave like a hot air balloon."

Step three: scientists test their hypothesis. (After all, what if the hypothesis is wrong? What if there really *are* werewolves? Gadzooks!) In testing their hypothesis, scientists follow a **procedure.** In the following experiments and activities, you will also follow a procedure. It is important to read through the instructions and set out all the needed materials *before* beginning the experiment. So sharpen your pencils, open your lab notebooks, and let's get started.

Did You Know?

Want to know more about paleontology? How about fumaroles, water pollution, or ham radios? While the Internet provides many handy and excellent resources, use caution. There is a lot of *mis*-information on the Internet, too. Why? Because anyone can post anything on the Internet, and no one is required to be correct. So, when you're looking for answers (and not just *any* answers, but the *right* answers), go to your local library. There you will find books written by *experts*. Having trouble finding just the right book? No problem. Just ask a reference librarian; they're there to help. After all, they're experts, too!

Werewolf Case at Midnight

Imagine it. You're a top-notch scientist, assigned to a baffling werewolf case at midnight on Waxberry Hill. Just as the howling begins and your scalp crawls with terror, the tent expands and floats off into the night. Are werewolves to blame, or is there a more obvious solution? As a top-notch scientist, it's your job to find out. . . .

MATERIALS

- thin plastic dry-cleaner bag (this is the tent)
  Note: The thinner and larger the bag, the better. Try evening gown–size dry-cleaner bags—they are about five-and-a-half feet long.
- 4 large paper clips
- lightweight fishing line (this is the leash, to keep your tent from flying away!)
- hair dryer

(CAUTION: Look over your shoulder now and then, just in case a werewolf is lurking. Don't let their howling unnerve you . . .)

PROCEDURE

This activity works best outside on a cool day or in the coolest part of the day. Do not do this activity if there is a breeze.

1. Reduce the size of the opening of the plastic bag (tent) so that it will act like the mouth of a hot air balloon. To do so, gather together small sections of the opening and firmly secure each section with a paper clip. When finished, the mouth of the plastic bag (tent) should be about twice the size of your fist.

2. Tie a long piece of fishing line to one of the paper clips so that your bag (tent) is retrievable.

3. Hold on to the opening of the plastic bag (tent) with one hand. Insert the hair dryer into the opening and turn it on. (Heat should be on

high. Be careful that you do not burn yourself or melt the bag.)

4. Once the bag (tent) is filled with hot air, turn off the hair dryer, hold on to the loose end of the fishing line, and release the bag (tent).

5. Watch in amazement as the bag (tent) floats up, up, and away!

6. Now determine what caused the bag (tent) to float. Werewolves? Hot air? Hmm . . . jot your conclusions in your lab notebook.

How does this work?

Air is composed of molecules. When air is cold, the molecules are close together and vibrate very little, making cold air dense and heavy.

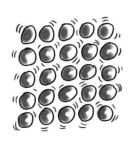

In hot air, however, the molecules vibrate quickly, bumping into one another like popping corn. Because each molecule needs more space to move, hot air expands, making hot air lighter and less dense than cold air.

Conclusion? Hot air tents are lighter than the surrounding cold air environment, so they float up, up, and away! (FYI: Werewolves, besides being shifty and dangerous creatures, are quite dense and therefore must stay on the ground.)

Those Poor Little Fish

It's tragic, quite tragic indeed. The water is polluted. The fish are counting on you to save the day! In this activity, you will test the pH of various water samples, just like Nell did. You will determine which water is safe for the fish and which water needs to be cleaned up, pronto!

MATERIALS

- 4 large baby-food jars with lids
- masking tape
- permanent marker
- measuring spoons
- tap water
- white vinegar
- baking soda
- water from a local river, stream, or lake
- purple cabbage
- pitcher
- measuring cup
- white coffee filters
- coffee strainer
- 1-quart jar with lid

- pencil
- scissors
- tweezers
- 2 clean, dry plates

PROCEDURE

1. Collect and prepare four water samples for testing. Prepare each sample as follows (using the tape and marker, label the jars clearly with numbers 1 through 4, and replace the lids as you go):

a) Jar #1: fill with tap water to about ¼ inch from the top.

b) Jar #2: pour in 1 tablespoon of white vinegar, then fill with tap water to about ¼ inch from the top.

c) Jar #3: fill halfway with tap water, add 1 teaspoon of baking soda, replace lid, and shake until dissolved. Finish filling with tap water to about ¼ inch from the top.

d) Jar #4: take a sample from a local river, stream, or lake. (See "Good Science Tip" on page 69.) Fill the jar to ¼ inch from the top.

2. Ask an adult to dice about 3 cups of cabbage. Place the cabbage in a pitcher and ask an adult to pour approximately 1½ cups of boiling water over the cabbage, enough to cover it completely. Let it soak for 30 minutes. (Note: cabbage juice can stain, so wear a lab coat!)

3. Place one coffee filter into the coffee strainer. Over a sink, pour the cabbage juice through the coffee filter/strainer into the 1-quart jar. (Be careful that clumps of cabbage don't fall— SPLAT!—into the strainer and stain your clothes!)

4. With the lid off the jar, let the juice cool completely. Once cool, replace the lid. Using a tape and marker, label the jar "Cabbage Juice," and date it. (**NOTE:** keep it refrigerated and discard after twenty-four hours.)

5. Draw some fish on white coffee filters. Each fish should be about 2 inches long. You'll need at least four fish, but make extra just in case. (Top-notch scientists are always prepared.) Cut out the fish with scissors.

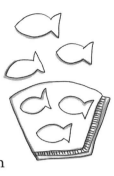

6. Using the tweezers, dunk one fish completely into the cabbage juice, and then place the wet fish on a plate to dry. Repeat with each fish. Allow fish to dry thoroughly.

7. Using a pencil, now label your four (dry) fish "#1," "#2," "#3," and "#4."

8. Again using the tweezers, dip the #1 fish into the #1 water sample. Lay the wet fish on another clean plate. Dip the #2 fish into the #2 water sample, and so on.

9. Important: record your results while the fish are still wet.

How Does This Work? (Reading the Results)

Scientists created the pH scale as a measurement of whether a substance is an acid or a base. The pH scale is numbered from 1 to 14. Acids range from 1 to 6. Bases range from 8 to 14. A neutral is 7.

pH Scale

1	2	3	4	5	6	7	8	9	10	11	12	13	14

More Acidic   ←   Neutral   →   More Basic

The pH scale also answers the questions *How acidic?* and *How basic?* For instance, a substance that scores a 2 on the pH scale is more acidic than a substance that scores a 4 or a 5. Likewise, a substance that scores a 14 on the pH scale is more basic than a substance that scores an 8 or a 9.

Well, you say, this is all very fascinating, really, but . . . what's that got to do with my poor little fish?

A most excellent question! You see, purple cabbage juice contains a purple pigment called *flavin*, which acts as a **pH indicator**. By dipping your paper fish into the cabbage juice, you created pH indicator fish! When mixed with acids, the pH indicator fish turn pink. When mixed with bases, they turn greenish yellow. But if a neutral liquid touches the indicator fish, the color doesn't change!

Now all you have to do is compare the color of your fish to the pH chart below. Determine which of the water samples were acids, bases, or neutrals. Were your fish swimming in "clean" or polluted water? Gadzooks! It's up to you to save the day! There's no time to lose!

pH Scale	1–2	3–4	5–6	7	8–9	10–11	12–14
Acid/Base?	Acid	Acid	Acid	Neutral	Base	Base	Base
Approximate Color of Fish	Pink	Dark Red	Violet	Violet-Blue	Blue-Green	Light Blue-Green	Greenish Yellow
Is the Water Polluted?*	Yes	Yes	Yes	No	Yes	Yes	Yes

*For this exercise, we will assume that anything other than a neutral pH indicates polluted water. In nature, this is not always the case.

For a full color pH scale, visit http://commons.wikimedia.org/wiki/File:PH_scale.png

BE A REAL-LIFE HERO!

Face it. Fish and other aquatic wildlife depend on us to keep their habitat clean. Why not be a real-life hero and help out your local waterway? Your efforts could save hundreds, maybe thousands, of lives! Here are some resources to get you started:

- www.kidsforsavingearth.org/ waterpollution/waterpollution.htm
- www.epa.gov/kids/water.htm
- www.epa.gov/adopt/earthday/index .html
- www.kiddyhouse.com/Themes/ Environ/Water.html
- www.oceansidecleanwaterprogram .org/kids.asp

Digging for Dinosaurs

In 1979, thirteen-year-old India Wood saw a bone sticking out of some layers of rock in Colorado. Being an amateur fossil hunter, India carefully excavated the bone. She identified it as the pelvic bone of an *Allosaurus,* a carnivorous dinosaur. Over the next several years, and with some help from the Denver Museum of Nature & Science, India excavated the entire *Allosaurus* skeleton (now on display at the museum). Way to go, India!

In this activity, not only will you create your own cool sedimentary layers, but you'll also practice digging for dinosaurs, just like India did!

MATERIALS

- 2-quart container with tight lid
- playground sand
- measuring spoons

- food coloring: green, yellow, blue, and red
- small plastic aquarium or similar clear container, approximately

11 by 7 by 8 inches (you can do an Internet search for "Critter Keeper")

- 8 to 10 small "fossils," such as shells, chicken bones (make sure they're clean!), or plastic dinosaurs
- small, clean paintbrush

PROCEDURE

1. Fill the 2-quart container about ⅔ full of sand.

2. Add 1½ teaspoons of green food coloring to the sand.

3. Replace the lid on the container and shake the sand for about 1 minute until the sand turns green.

4. Pour half of the green sand into the plastic aquarium. Place some of your fossils here and there on the sand, and then pour in the remaining green sand.

5. Repeat steps 1–4 with each of the yellow, blue, and red food colorings.

6. Record your observations. (Can you see the different stratification layers?)

7. Using the paintbrush, go on a dig. Carefully brush away the sand until you—*gasp!*—stumble upon a fossil! Continue to brush away the excess sand until the fossil is completely exposed. (If you need to scoop out some sand from your aquarium, go ahead. Just be sure you don't disturb or remove your amazing fossil.)

8. Draw a site map in your notebook.

Tip: Looking down from above, draw a picture of your fossil exactly where it lies. Label your fossil and indicate what color layer you found it in.

DINO DIG MAP

TRICERATOPS   BRACHIOSAURUS

ALLOSAURUS

2' SCALE

9. Carefully remove the fossil and put it on display in your private museum collection!

DIG THIS!

Are you itching to be the next India Wood? Whether you're after an *Allosaurus* or a trilobite, here is some information on clubs, organizations, museums, and summer digs to get you started. Dig it?

CLUBS AND ORGANIZATIONS

Paleontological Society: www.paleosoc.org

Western Interior Paleontological Society:
www.wipsppc.com

Paleontological Societies and Clubs:
www.paleo.cc/kpaleo/paleorgs.htm

**Ozark Earth Science Gem,
Mineral & Fossil Club, Arkansas:**
www.ozarkearthscience.org

Florida Fossil Hunters:
www.floridafossilhunters.com/Kids.htm

**Delaware Valley Paleontological Society,
Pennsylvania:** dvps.essentrix.net

SUMMER DIGS AND PROGRAMS

Wyoming Dinosaur Center & Dig Sites:
www.wyodino.org

Dinosaur State Park, Connecticut:
www.dinosaurstatepark.org

Paleo Park, Wyoming: www.paleopark.com

Judith River Dinosaur Institute, Montana:
www.montanadinosaurdigs.com
(minimum age: 14)

Museum of Western Colorado:
www.dinodigs.org

PaleoWorld Research Foundation, Montana:
www.paleoworld.org

MUSEUMS

American Museum of Natural History, New York:
www.amnh.org/exhibitions/permanent/fossilhalls

Denver Museum of Nature & Science, Colorado:
www.dmns.org/exhibitions/current-exhibitions/
prehistoric-journey

Paleontological Education Preserve, Florida:
www.paleopreserve.org

Hamming It Up with Morse Code

About 170 years ago, no one knew how to transmit voices (or music) over the radio. (Heck, no one even knew that radio waves *existed*.) It was impossible to communicate quickly with someone who lived thousands of miles away. (Remember—no e-mail, no faxes, no text messaging, no telephones . . . egads!) Fortunately, a man named Samuel Morse (1791–1872) developed a code, called *Morse code*, which enabled people to communicate quickly over long distances. This communication system was called the *telegraph*.

MORSE CODE	
A .–	S ...
B –...	T –
C –.–.	U ..–
D –..	V ...–
E .	W .––
F ..–.	X –..–
G ––.	Y –.––
H	Z ––..
I ..	1 .––––
J .–––	2 ..–––
K –.–	3 ...––
L .–..	4 ....–
M ––	5 .....
N –.	6 –....
O –––	7 ––...
P .––.	8 –––..
Q ––.–	9 ––––.
R .–.	0 –––––

Morse code doesn't require the human voice or even a piece of paper. Instead, it uses a pattern of short and long beeps called *dots* and *dashes*. Each letter is assigned its own pattern of dots and dashes. For instance, the letter K is composed of a dash, a dot, and a dash.

It is written as follows: —·—, and it sounds like "beeeep, beep, beeeep." A trained listener would know that he or she was hearing the letter K.

When Nell sent Drake a secret message, she wrote it in Morse code. You, too, can write messages in Morse code. Use / to indicate the end of a letter, // for the end of a word, and /// for the end of a sentence. Practice your detective skills by decoding the following:

..../._/__/...//._/._././/_._./___/___/._..///

If you have access to the Internet, you can actually *hear* what Morse code sounds like. Go to http://morsecode.scphillips.com/translator.html, and type a message in the "input text" box. Click "Play Sound," and then click "Submit." Pretty nifty, eh?

You can also practice your skills using the online Morse code machine at www.boyslife.org/games/online-games/575/morse-code-machine.

SHH . . . DETECTIVES AT WORK!

In a tight spot? Need to signal your detective partner, but your archenemy is listening in? No worries! Using Morse code, you and your friends can silently signal one another with flashlights. Simply cover and uncover the light in a series of long and short exposures. You'll outsmart any Frisco out there who might be spying!

HAM IT UP!

Ham radio (also known as *amateur radio*) began as a hobby in the early 1900s. Anyone who had the right equipment could transmit and receive radio communications. The catch? Ham radio operators (known as *hams*) could communicate only using Morse code. They filled the airwaves with Morse code chatter!

Nowadays, though, hams not only get to twirl knobs and press buttons, but they get to talk to people all over the world, and say stuff like, "CQ CQ CQ, this is KA7, blah blah blah, over!" ("CQ

CQ CQ" is a very cool way of saying, "Hello! Can anyone hear me?") It's the perfect hobby for amateur science detective geniuses! There is no minimum age requirement to be a ham. Just pass the test, and you're good to go. (And since almost all hams know Morse code, you can even practice your spy skills!) Interested? Here are some websites to get you started:

- www.hello-radio.org
- www.belmont.k12.ma.us/
  class_pages/laroche/ham_radio/
  acquainted/index.htm
- www.arrl.org
- www.k3nhc.org
- www.south.mccsc.edu/~nrapp/ham/
  index.htm

DID YOU KNOW?

When disaster strikes, often cell phones, landlines, and computers won't operate. Communication becomes difficult, if not impossible. Enter ham radios. Come hurricane or ice storm, hams can communicate even when other lines of communication are broken. Over the decades, hams have saved countless lives during emergencies, calling for help when no one else could, sometimes even using Morse code! Hams were put to the test again when Hurricane Katrina hit New Orleans in August 2005. These ham heroes communicated with the Red Cross and other emergency organizations, helping to coordinate rescue efforts. Way to go, hams! (See www.ares.org for more.)

3 1901 05716 1335